CHOOSE YOUR OWN ADVENTURE®

Kids Love Reading
Choose Your Own Adventure®!

"It's like a new book every time I pick it up."
Quin Carpenter, age 9

"I love all the riddles they are so fun! I can't wait to finish it at home, I did not know there were so many ways to go!"
Charlotte Young, age 9

"You never know what's going to happen next!"
Skylar Stoudt, age 8

"I like how it was me choosing what to do and how it felt to actually be the main character."
Wilson Stack, age 9

"These books are the best! They make it so you're the character."
Josslyn Jewett, age 9

Illustrated by Fian Arroyo
Book design by Stacey Boyd, Big Eyedea Visual Design
For information regarding permission, write to:

CHOOSECO

P.O. Box 46, Waitsfield, Vermont 05673
www.cyoa.com

A DRAGONLARK BOOK

ISBN: 1-937133-72-9
EAN: 978-1-937133-72-6

Names: Ridyard, Sarah Bounty, author. | Arroyo, Fian, illustrator.
Title: Mermaid Island / by Sarah Bounty Ridyard ; illustrated by Fian Arroyo.
Other Titles: Choose your own adventure. Dragonlarks.
Description: Waitsfield, Vermont : Chooseco, [2020] | Interest age level: 005-008. |
Summary: "YOU are a magical mermaid who has lived her entire life in an underwater palace. You celebrate and protect all species under the sea. Princess Island and Prince Island, the very best royal summer camps, are right nearby. Ever since you were a little mermaid you have dreamed of leaving your underwater home and joining the land princesses. Will YOU leave your comfortable palace under the sea and teach the land princesses and princes the importance of protecting the planet and our oceans?"-- Provided by publisher.
Identifiers: ISBN 9781937133726 | ISBN 1937133729
Subjects: LCSH: Mermaids--Juvenile fiction. | Princes--Juvenile fiction. | Princesses--Juvenile fiction. | Environmental protection--Juvenile fiction. | CYAC: Mermaids--Fiction. | Princes--Fiction. | Princesses--Fiction. | Environmental protection--Fiction. | LCGFT: Action and adventure fiction. | Choose-your-own stories.
Classification: LCC PZ7.1.R539 Mer 2020 | DDC [Fic]--dc23

Published simultaneously in the United States and Canada

Printed in Malaysia

10 9 8 7 6 5 4 3 2 1

CHOOSE YOUR OWN ADVENTURE®

Mermaid Island

BY SARAH BOUNTY RIDYARD

ILLUSTRATED BY FIAN ARROYO

A DRAGONLARK BOOK

For Ellie

WATCH OUT!
THIS BOOK IS DIFFERENT
from every book you've ever read.

Do not read this book from the first page
through to the last page.
Instead, start on page 1 and read until you
come to your first choice. Then turn to the
page shown and see what happens.

When you come to the end of a story,
you can go back and start again.
Every choice leads to a new adventure.

Good luck!

You are a mermaid. That's right—a real, live, mermaid! You have a beautiful tail and everything. Your name is Sirena Ondine. You live under the sea (of course!). You live with your parents and your younger sister, Marina Phoebe.

"Sirena, please listen carefully," your mother says to you. "Your father and I have an important event to attend. We are going to the Beach Ball." The Beach Ball is a very fancy event for royals who live under the sea.

"I know, Mom! You've told us a thousand times," you say with an eye roll. "'Stay home! Don't forget to feed the fish! Make sure you keep your rooms clean,'" you say to your mom. Even mermaids have to clean their rooms.

"That's right, Sirena. And keep an eye on your sister. We will be back tomorrow morning," your mother says.

"Of course," you say. "Have a good time!" You give your parents a hug.

Turn to the next page.

You and your family live in a palace under the sea. The palace is near an island. It's a very special island. Every summer, the island hosts a camp for princesses.

You watch as your parents start to swim off into the open ocean. Speaking of Marina, where has she gone to? You realize she isn't here to say goodbye.

Before you can think too much about your sister, you hear the whir of a motorboat. You look up at the sparkling blue water above you.

Go on to the next page.

You are used to these boats coming and going. It is especially busy now, at the start of the summer. You have watched the princesses be dropped off for camp at this island year after year. You wish you could join them, but you know the camp is only for princesses on land.

Suddenly the boat stops, and the motor turns off. It has not reached the island but stopped in the open ocean. How unusual!

Turn to the next page.

You swim closer to the boat. Maybe they ran out of gas and they need help?

As you are watching the boat, something silver is tossed overboard. It lands in the water with a loud splash. It sinks to the ocean floor. You hear the motor start up again. The boat speeds off toward the island again.

"Litterbarnacles!" you say to yourself. "Or, I suppose, litterbugs since they live on land." You laugh to yourself. What was thrown into the ocean now?

Go on to the next page.

As you start to swim toward the silver thing, you hear something. You hear a voice from behind you.

"Sirena! Come here, I want to show you something!" your sister Marina calls to you. She loves to show you things—a starfish one day, a piece of coral the next. Usually it's something ordinary that you have seen before. Something about her voice this time tells you it may be different.

If you decide to swim toward the dropped object, turn to page 7.

If you decide to return to your sister and see what she wants to show you, turn to page 8.

You swim to the object and realize it is a silver trophy cup. It is beautiful! The trophy would be a great addition to your collection of sea treasures. You keep these treasures hidden from your sister in a secret corner of the ocean.

You grab the silver cup and take it over to your special spot. You make sure Marina doesn't follow you. You notice the water bubbling over by the shore. What could that be? The trophy is heavy. You're not sure you want to go check it out before you drop it off in your hiding place.

If you decide to investigate the bubbling water, turn to page 12.

If you decide to continue to your secret corner, turn to page 29.

You return to your sister, who shows you a handwritten note.

Go on to the next page.

It says:

You may search
for a hundred years
but never find
the Cabin Cup again,
Princesses!
Signed,

the Princes
of Prince Island

The Cabin Cup? That must be what you saw falling from the boat! You tell Marina about seeing the trophy being thrown from the boat.

You have to tell the princesses where their Cup is so they can get it back. Or you could tell the princes to retrieve their garbage?

"Prince Island? Isn't that on the other side of the Sea Kelp Forest?" says Marina.

Turn to the next page.

She's right, the way to Prince Island is through the scary and dark Sea Kelp Forest. The way to Princess Island, on the other hand, is just up the Royal River, not far at all. You're not sure the princesses will be able to help you, though.

If you choose to swim up the Royal River into Princess Island and tell the princesses about the Cup, turn to page 14.

If you would rather swim toward Prince Island and tell those princes to put their garbage somewhere else, turn to page 26.

You bravely answer the Garbage.

"It is I, Sirena Ondine! And my sister, Marina Phoebe. We wish to pass through here."

The Garbage considers this and swirls around. You grab Marina's hand. You can tell you don't want to be on his bad side.

Turn to page 27.

12

You swim over to the bubbling water. You realize it is a waterfall pouring into the ocean from the island! You can't believe you have never noticed this before.

You decide to swim behind the waterfall.

Turn to page 63.

You and Marina swim upriver. It is a slow journey, but you do it together. You see different kinds of plant and animal life as you move from the saltwater to the freshwater.

Up ahead you see a fork in the river. One side looks spooky and dark but the water is nice and deep, and the other side is bright and full of happy fish, with shallow water. Deep water is better for swimming; shallow water means you might get stuck.

If you choose the spooky, dark, and deep fork, turn to page 16.

If you choose the bright, inviting, and shallow fork, turn to page 41.

You and Marina swim up the spooky, dark fork of the river.

"I'm scared," Marina says, swimming close to you. "What if we can't find our way back?"

"It will be okay, Marina, I promise. All rivers lead back to the ocean," you tell her, and hold her hand.

Go on to the next page.

You see something silvery shimmering up ahead in the water. What could that be?

Marina says, "This is a sign we shouldn't go any farther!"

If you choose to investigate the silver shimmer, turn to page 30.

If you decide to turn back down the river toward the ocean, turn to page 46.

18

The turtles are so happy to see Shelly! You can tell she is a popular turtle.

Shelly swims playfully around you and your sister. She wraps a flipper around each of you and whispers in your ear, "You are welcome back any time to visit!"

You and your turtle friends enjoy many years of friendship, and avoiding the Garbage together.

The End

You decide not to go through the dark and confusing Sea Kelp Forest. You and your sister head north to navigate around it. It is larger than you remember. This may be a long swim.

Turn the page to see a map of where you are going! Then turn to page 23.

PRINCESS ISLAND

WITCH'S

RIDING CENTER

ARTS & CRAFTS

BURIAL GROUND

ARCHERY

SINGING CIRCLE

LAKE LOUISE

CABINS

ROYAL RIV

MAIN LODGE

GARBAG
MONSTE

WATER SPORTS

SEA KELP FOREST

PRINCE ISLAND

ARCHERY

CABINS

ARTS & CRAFTS

CABINS

MAIN LODGE

CABINS

WATER SPORTS

There are vibrant plants and animals of all types. You look around above and below the water and take in this magical place.

A unicorn pauses to take a drink of water. You watch with wide eyes. You decide you could stay here for a while . . . .

The End

As you and Marina come around the edge of the Sea Kelp Forest, something menacing comes into view. As you get closer, you see it is a giant vortex of garbage. Who would dump so much trash in the sea? It is made up of millions of tiny pieces of plastic and other garbage. All of the small pieces of trash have collected here to create a Great Vortex of Garbage, swirling endlessly in the ocean. The sea around it looks so unhealthy.

Turn to the next page.

As you approach it, the garbage swirls to make a giant face. A booming voice comes from the mouth of the Great Vortex of Garbage.

"WHO DARES TO DISTURB THE GREAT VORTEX OF GARBAGE?" it thunders, echoing in the sea.

Marina looks terrified. Should you answer the garbage or just get out of here right away?

If you answer the Garbage, turn to page 11.

If you grab Marina's hand and swim away as fast as you can, turn to page 52.

Prince Island is far to the east, beyond the Sea Kelp Forest.

"We'll swim around, not through," you tell Marina, because you know she is scared of the dark sea kelp. It grows together in thick knots and the sun from above the water hardly peeks through.

You begin swimming with your sister. Prince Island is so far away you don't see it. Marina falls behind. You look back and see her arms are dangling by her sides and she's not moving forward.

"I'm tired, Sirena," she tells you. "This is far."
Sea Kelp Forest is ahead of you.

The swim through the forest looks to be short, but it is dark and mysterious. Swimming around the forest looks like it will take a long time.

If you choose to go around the Sea Kelp Forest, turn to page 19.

If you choose to go through the Sea Kelp Forest, turn to page 47.

As he swirls, you notice a sea turtle trapped by the Garbage. She has a plastic ring around her flipper and is stuck in the Garbage. Thinking quickly, you devise a plan to save the sea turtle from the Garbage.

"We also need our friend . . . uh, Shelly. The turtle."

"ONLY IF YOU BRING ME MORE GARBAGE," thunders the Garbage.

Turn to the next page.

You are torn. Do you bring more garbage to this monster, hoping to save the turtle, or do you try to get away without adding to the waste?

If you decide to obey the Garbage's command and BRING MORE GARBAGE, turn to page 36.

If you stand up to the Garbage and demand he let you and the turtle leave without adding more trash to him, turn to page 64.

You place the trophy on top of your collection. You have all sorts of things hidden here—fishing lures, interesting shells, unique rocks. The trophy fits right in. You soon forget all about the mysterious way it came into your life. You never figure out why it was dropped off—but some mysteries are never meant to be solved (right?).

The End

You swim closer to the silvery, swirling object. As you approach it, you realize it is not an object at all, but the ghost of a river otter! He motions for you and Marina to follow him to the edge where the river meets the land.

Follow the river otter and turn to page 32.

You and your sister swim to the edge of the river, and the river otter ghost hops out of the water onto the bank.

You pop your heads up above the surface of the water to see where he is going.

A group of camp counselors from Princess Island are standing near the water.

"Did you hear the latest gossip about the King and Queen of Orion? Apparently they have bought another golden goose statue," says one of the counselors with a high ponytail and a fresh manicure.

"Another one? Don't they already have seven?!" says another counselor.

"You know they have a secret stash of treasure, don't you? It's supposedly right here on this island."

Turn to page 34.

They are so engrossed in their conversation they do not even see the river otter ghost as he scurries away.

Marina does not spy on humans as often as you do. She is wide-eyed and interested. Would she be too scared if you asked them a question?

If you try to get the counselors' attention by calling to them and asking if they saw the river otter ghost, go on to the next page.

If you decide to keep quiet and eavesdrop a little bit on what they are talking about, turn to page 48.

go on to the next page.

turn to page 48.

"Hey!" you shout to the counselors and interrupt their conversation.

"Excuse me? Are you campers? The Royal River is off limits, you should know that. Who is your counselor? You need to head back to your cabin." A counselor with the blue shirt starts walking over to you.

"We can't do that," says Marina as she slaps her tail on the water to make a point.

Turn to page 37.

You decide to help Shelly the turtle, even if it means giving the Garbage what he wants.

You and Marina think the perfect piece of garbage to give the monster would be the shiny Cup you saw drop from the boat. You return to where it landed and pick it up from the ocean floor.

Turn to page 42.

"We are looking for someone to help us. Look at this note." You add a slap of your tail as well, as you hand the note to the counselor. "Some boys dropped a trophy down into the ocean and left this."

The counselors thank you for coming to them and apologize to you for the princes leaving the Cabin Cup on the ocean floor. They promise to help to get the Cup out of the ocean.

Turn to page 39.

You and Marina head home. The next day, a boat returns and you can see the boys retrieving the Cabin Cup using a fishing pole. Not only do they retrieve the Cup, but the boys' counselors make the princes clean up all the trash from the shores of Princess Island as payback for stealing the Cabin Cup.

The princes spend a long day gathering up any trash from the beaches and rocky shores, making sure it won't end up in your home.

The princesses help out and it becomes an annual tradition, making the ocean healthier and happier for all!

The End

You and Marina swim up the bright and inviting fork of the river. You see some girls about your age in the water ahead of you. There is something unusual about them, though. Where their tails should be they have two limbs instead! Oh, right. They have legs. These must be the princesses of Princess Island!

You would love to talk to them. Maybe you should pop your heads above water so you don't scare them. But you are really curious about their feet and toes. Maybe you should grab a princess's foot while you have this chance!

If you grab one of the princesses' toes to get their attention (and to see what all the fuss about feet is), turn to page 55.

If you pop your head above water to talk to the princesses, turn to page 69.

The Cup is very heavy but you and Marina bring it back to the Garbage. He accepts it and frees Shelly!

Go on to the next page.

Shelly looks very happy to be free of the Great Vortex of Garbage. She gestures for you to follow her, off in the opposite direction of Prince Island. Should you go with her? Or stick with your original plan to go to Prince Island and complain about the garbage they dropped? It might be the only way to stop the monster from getting even bigger!

If you choose to follow Shelly, turn to page 45.

If you choose to go on to Prince Island to tell them where to put their garbage, turn to page 72.

You and Marina follow Shelly the turtle. You start to get a little nervous that the swim is taking a long time. Where is she leading you? But then you round a corner around a coral reef and suddenly you are surrounded by the most beautiful sea life, including all of Shelly the turtle's friends and family.

Turn to page 18.

You and Marina decide the freshwater life is not for you. You hightail it back downriver to the open ocean, where you are free and where you are home!

You head back to the palace. You arrive just in time to feed your pet fish and clean your room before tucking yourself into your sea bed.

The End

You enter the Sea Kelp Forest. The forest is dark and dense, with no sunlight reaching through the waves of kelp. You can barely see your hand in front of you.

You realize you will never be able to make it back out of the Sea Kelp Forest. You are trapped in the tangle of plants.

The End

48

You and Marina quietly approach the shore, keeping your ears open. You overhear the counselors whispering:

"They say the treasure has never been seen again!"

"But where could it be?"

"Supposedly it is at the bottom of Lake Louise, but it's just a rumor . . ."

Go on to the next page.

"Lake Louise? That's just up the river from here!"

"How could anyone get to the bottom of it? It is so deep!"

You know where Lake Louise is. You and Marina could swim to the bottom of it yourselves for the treasure. But maybe you should talk to the counselors about this plan?

If you decide to look for this treasure in Lake Louise, turn to the next page.

If you choose to talk to the counselors, turn to page 54.

You and your sister quietly dip beneath the water and continue your swim upstream to Lake Louise.

Along the way you encounter a cranky river porpoise. He tells you there is no treasure and you shouldn't listen to rumors.

Disappointed, you and Marina have no choice but to return to the salty life of the ocean.

The End

You and Marina swim away from the scary Garbage. You know in your heart you must protect the sea from such a terrible fate. You head home, where you devote yourself to studying and eventually, you become an environmental engineer. You invent a solar-powered sea robot to collect the garbage from the ocean and recycle it. No one will ever be threatened by the Great Vortex of Garbage again!

The End

"Excuse me!" you interrupt the counselors, and they immediately stop their conversation.

They are surprised to see you.

"I couldn't help but overhear, what is this treasure you are talking about? Also, do you know anything about a large, silver trophy cup?"

The counselors whisper among themselves for a moment, and one steps forward to ask what you know about the Cup.

If you decide to tell the counselors where the Cup is and forget about the treasure, turn to page 58.

If you decide to ask them to tell you about the treasure in exchange for you telling them about the Cup, turn to page 74.

You stay below the surface of the water and swim close to the princesses. You give Marina a wild grin, and then you reach through the water and grab the toes of the princess closest to you.

Feet sure are weird! Like hands, but so much less useful, and terrible for swimming.

Turn to page 57.

Immediately you can tell you have made a mistake. The princess you grabbed screams and starts dashing toward the shore of the river.

"Something grabbed me!" you can hear her say, muffled under the water. "It must be the River Monster!"

The other princesses begin to scream and head for shore as well.

"Hey, wait! I need to talk to you!" you shout in their direction, but it is too late.

You can tell the princesses will never get in the water again, for fear of the River Monster grabbing their feet.

The End

You decide you should tell the counselors about the trophy right now.

"There is a huge silver cup at the bottom of the ocean right now. It was left by some littering princes. They also left a note."

Go on to the next page.

You pass a note to the counselor closest to you. The counselors chatter among themselves. Clearly this Cup is very important to them. One of them, with a different color shirt, speaks for the group.

"We can get a boat out there tomorrow morning, but we need help finding the exact location of the Cup. Can you help us?" says the counselor.

"Yes, of course!" you and Marina agree.

Turn to page 61.

The next day you swim to the shore and guide the boat to the location of the Cup. A team of princess campers in scuba gear swim down to the bottom and bring the Cabin Cup to the surface.

Having the princesses in the water in scuba gear makes you realize how much you all have in common. You know you will be lifelong friends with these girls and look forward to helping out as the camp enhances its Oceanography courses and Marine activities over the years to come.

The End

You swim behind the waterfall, and you are in an enchanted place! Magical butterflies float through the air, and the water is filled with amazing colorful rocks and more creatures than you have ever seen.

Turn to page 22.

"I will not add to your swirling vortex of mess!" you call to the Garbage. You do not want to see more of your ocean home full of garbage so you stand up to the Garbage, and tell him, "There is no way I will do that."

The Garbage swirls, thinking. "Hmmm," he says. "Okay. You can have the turtle, but leave the plastic. And never come back here again!" he thunders after a pause.

"Fine with us!" says Marina as she frees the turtle from the trash and pulls her away.

You leave the Garbage, and take Shelly the turtle and Marina to Prince Island.

Go on to the next page.

Shelly the turtle motions for you to grab on to her shell. It turns out that sea turtles are fast! She speeds you over to Prince Island in no time at all.

Turn to the next page.

As you approach the island you can see a dock with boats next to it, and a sandy beach.

You see a group of boys on the dock by the boats. Maybe these boys are the same ones who dropped the shiny Cup into the ocean? On the beach, you see one boy standing alone. He looks upset.

If you choose to go talk to the boys by the boats, turn to page 68.

If you decide to go see if you can help the upset boy, turn to page 83.

68

You decide to head to the boats to see if you can talk to the boys. As you swim toward the boats, you notice that the sky over the ocean has gotten very dark. The boys rush to take cover, and you can tell a pouring rain has started on land.

Turn to page 82.

You pop your head up above water and see four girls around you. You talk to the girls and tell them about the note your sister found, and the shiny object you saw the boys throw into the ocean.

The girls are intrigued.

"The original Cabin Cup!" they exclaim. "I thought it was lost forever!"

You offer to the princesses that you can get the Cup for them, because you can swim to the bottom of the ocean.

"I'm not sure this is such a good idea," says Marina. "Do we really want to get involved in this?"

Turn to the next page.

Marina is right, you should not get involved in this human world and its problems.

"You can find the Cup on the bottom of the ocean, just off the southern shore of the island. Due south, half a nautical mile," you tell the princesses.

You and Marina head back down the river toward the ocean. That's enough adventure for one day!

The End

You and Marina swim over to Prince Island. Now you will have to tell the boys that they must get their trophy back from the Garbage.

The rest of the journey to the island is relatively uneventful and you arrive at the edge of Prince Island quickly.

You see a group of boys on the dock and you swim over to them.

Go on to the next page.

"Hey!" You pop your head up above the water and call to them.

The boys come over to you.

"Are you the boys who threw a trophy into the sea?" you ask.

"Depends who's asking!" says a tough-looking boy. You realize he doesn't see that you are a mermaid. Maybe you should take this chance to really give him a surprise.

If you decide to ask the boys nicely to take care of the ocean, turn to page 77.

If you decide to make up a story to tell the boys to scare them, turn to page 80.

"Before I tell you that, tell me more about the treasure," you say confidently to the counselors.

The counselors tell you a story, a legend they say, of a secret stash of treasure at the bottom of Lake Louise, on Princess Island. The treasure has been there since before Princess Island was founded, and is supposedly guarded in a cave by a water kelpie—a special kind of lake monster with the ability to shift shapes.

Turn to page 76.

You are intrigued by the secret treasure. You tell the counselors the basic location of the Cabin Cup and give them a few landmarks so they should be able to find it. The counselors thank you and leave you and Marina.

"I'm ready to go home!" says Marina.

Turn to page 78.

"The ocean is our home, just like you live in your houses on land. You wouldn't throw trash in your yard would you? Where you would have to see it every day and where it would bother the animals and plants?" you ask the boys. You show them seagulls on the shore with plastic bags stuck around their feet, and a seal with a flipper stuck in a plastic bottle.

"We had no idea!" the tough-looking boy says. The other boys agree, and pledge to help keep the ocean clean. The boys round up a crew and head out to get their trophy back and tackle the Garbage.

The boys pledge to be good stewards of the ocean and hold annual ocean cleanups to prevent the Garbage from taking over again.

The End

Having a little sister can be a bit of a drag sometimes! You realize she isn't up for the same amount of adventure that you are. You decide it's time to head back to the familiar sea and you and Marina spend the rest of the day playing ping pong (her favorite game). You are a good big sister!

The End

"Well, your trophy landed on a terrible sea monster, just so you know. The, uh, Horrendous Hag," you say, thinking quickly. "He is an awful and angry monster. He has claws as big as his body, and gigantic fins. And he is coming to get you!" The boys look terrified.

Just as you finish your story, a loud splash erupts behind you! A giant fin pokes up from under the water. The boys run screaming back to their cabins.

Marina chuckles as the boys run off; the fin was just her poking her tail up from underwater! Silly boys. You and Marina share a laugh; having a little sister can be a lot of fun.

The End

This is not a rainstorm, it's a typhoon! You will have to continue your quest another time. The land dwellers don't like to get wet, and it could be days before this storm ends.

The End

You swim toward the beach to see what the problem is.

When you get close enough, you see there is an injured seagull on the beach. The boy is looking at it.

"Can you help him? My name is Brian," says the boy.

Luckily, all mermaids know just which kinds of sea plants are used for healing. You help the boy heal the bird.

You can tell this boy understands how important nature and the ocean are.

Turn to the next page.

As the bird flies away, you tell Brian about the trophy in the ocean, and about the Garbage monster. You tell him how upset you are to see your home so dirty.

Brian agrees to help you with getting the trophy out of the ocean. Brian's father owns a large boat, and the next day he helps you get the trophy and clean up the garbage. They agree to help you clean up other garbage in the ocean, too, and you realize you have made a friend for life!

The End

ABOUT THE ARTIST

Fian Arroyo, with his creative mind and quick draw, has been creating award-winning illustrations and character designs for his clients, including many Fortune-500 companies, in the advertising, editorial, toy and game, and publishing markets for over twenty years. What began as something to do until he found out what he wanted to be when he grew up has blossomed into a full-time detour from getting a "real job." He has had the pleasure of working with companies such as *U.S. News & World Report,* ABC Television Network, KFC, Taco Bell, *The Los Angeles Times,* SC Johnson, the United States Postal Service, and many more.

Originally from San Juan, Puerto Rico, Fian grew up traveling the world as a U.S. Army brat. He graduated from Texas State University in 1986 with a BFA in Commercial Art, then moved to Miami, Florida, where he began his freelance illustration career. In 2009, he relocated from Miami Beach to the breathtaking mountains of Asheville, North Carolina, where he lives with his wife and two kids.

ABOUT THE AUTHOR

Sarah Bounty Ridyard has spent most of her life enjoying the outdoors in New England, with a brief stint in Colorado while she obtained a master's degree. She pursued an education in Environmental Engineering to balance her love of nature with a desire to improve the daily lives of people. Sarah has worked in a variety of different positions as an engineer, ranging from an environmental nonprofit to consulting on municipal water projects in Boston. Her professional focus has always been protecting and preserving water supplies, and what makes her happiest (besides a cup of tea and a good book) is to share her passion for the environment with those around her. She currently lives in Connecticut, with her husband, daughter, and the world's best cat.

For games, activities, and other fun stuff, or to write to Sarah, visit us online at CYOA.com